MW01000101

A LITTLE SPOT OF HAPPINESS

Written & Illustrated
by Diane Alber

To my children, Ryan and Anna:

You grow my HAPPINESS SPOT every day!

This book belongs to:

_____

_____

_____

Hi! I'm a HAPPINESS SPOT!

I'm here to help you feel JOY and spread
HAPPINESS to others!

Did you know one person has the power to
grow hundreds of HAPPINESS SPOTS all with one KIND act?
Let me show you!

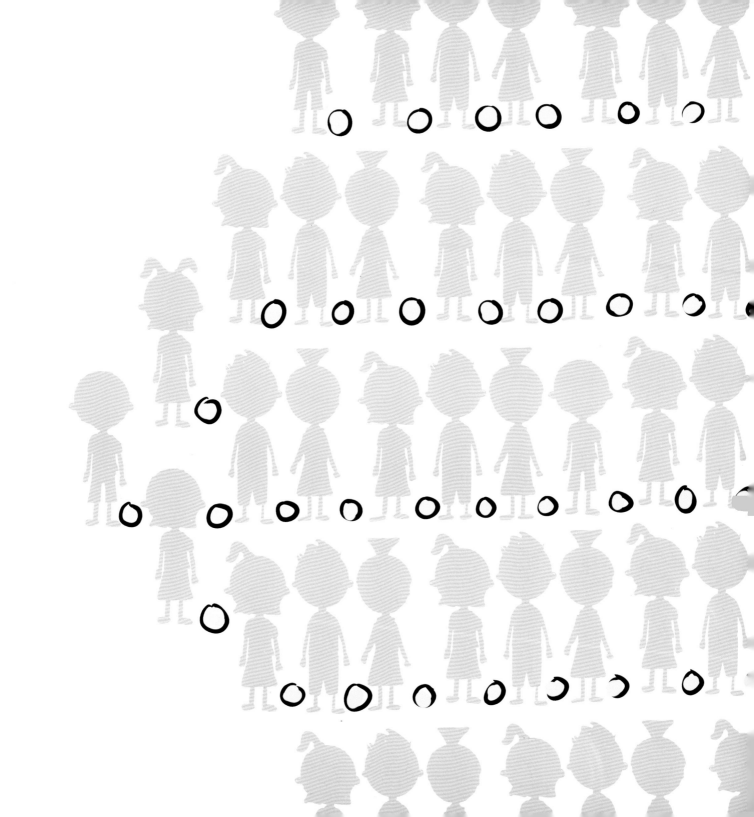

It can start with YOU being KIND and helping Jimmy up when he falls down...

Because you were KIND, Jimmy wants to be KIND, too, so he shares his toys with Lucy!

You can use several SPOTS to
help a HAPPINESS SPOT grow, too!

LOVE, CONFIDENCE, and PEACEFUL are some of the HAPPIEST SPOTS I know!

LOVE

CONFIDENCE

PEACEFUL

Think about all the people you LOVE in your life,
and all the people who LOVE you!

LOVE can grow a HAPPINESS SPOT.

Create ART. Even if you feel you are not good at it, when you create something from the HEART, it can be one of the greatest gifts to give.

CREATING can grow a HAPPINESS SPOT!

When you believe in yourself,
it is easier to see the good in others.

CONFIDENCE can grow a
HAPPINESS SPOT.

Learn how to manage your emotions.

When you are CALM, it can help
to CALM people around you!

Being PEACEFUL can grow
a HAPPINESS SPOT!

Another way to spread HAPPINESS is with
GRATITUDE!

GRATITUDE

is being thankful and showing appreciation
with KINDNESS!

Try writing three things you are thankful for EVERY DAY. It's so easy to do, and it can start your day in a positive way!

Write a thank-you note, too!

It lets people know that you are grateful for them!

Being THANKFUL can
grow a HAPPINESS SPOT.

Take time to enjoy all the things around you.
Point out all the beautiful things to others, too!

APPRECIATION can grow a
HAPPINESS SPOT.

SMILE!

Making yourself smile, tricks your brain into thinking happy thoughts! Go ahead and try it!

Did you know when you SMILE, it makes other people want to smile, too?

SMILING can grow a
HAPPINESS SPOT.

Create something NEW....

and help others do the same!

IMAGINATION can grow a
HAPPINESS SPOT.

Take care of the planet. You can recycle or plant a tree!
It doesn't look like much now, but every little
action matters.

CARING can grow a HAPPINESS SPOT.

Find a great book! You might learn something new.
Use your imagination and experience new places!

READING can grow a HAPPINESS SPOT.

Sometimes you just need a
reminder to spread HAPPINESS!

So wear a SPOT on your hand and every time you
SPOT me, think of a happy thought and spread

HAPPINESS!

SP🔘T CARD

Monday	Tuesday	Wednesday

Thursday	Friday	Saturday	Sunday

How did you grow a HAPPINESS SPOT?

Mark a spot on every day you grow a HAPPINESS SPOT!
Can you spread HAPPINESS all week?